HENRY DAVID THOREAU
WALDEN

text selections by STEVE LOWE

illustrations by ROBERT SABUDA

PHILOMEL BOOKS/NEW YORK

To my son, Michael
S. L.

For Dale
R. S.

Grateful acknowledgment is made to the Thoreau Lyceum,
Concord, Massachusetts, and the Thoreau Museum, Concord,
Massachusetts, for their assistance and guidance in gathering and verifying
factual information for this book.

A NOTE ABOUT THE TEXT:

The selections in this picture book are comprised of Henry David Thoreau's
own words. Great care was taken in choosing the extracts to maintain
the essence and intent of Thoreau's original piece.
Ellipses are used to indicate missing words that may have referred to
parts of the original not contained in these pages.
The last line of pages 5, 9, and 16 appear as semicolons in Thoreau's
original and appear as periods in this book.
—S. L.

Compilation copyright © 1990 by Steven Lowe
Introduction © 1990 Philomel Books, a division of The Putnam & Grosset Book Group
Illustrations copyright © 1990 by Robert Sabuda. All rights reserved.
Published by Philomel Books, a division of The Putnam & Grosset Book Group,
200 Madison Avenue, New York, NY 10016. Published simultaneously in Canada.
Printed in Hong Kong by South China Printing Co. (1988) Ltd.
Book design by Christy Hale
Library of Congress Cataloging-in-Publication Data
Lowe, Steve. Walden.
Summary: In this illustrated adaptation of Thoreau's famous work, a man retreats
into the woods and discovers the joys of solitude and nature.
[1. Nature—Fiction. 2. Forests and forestry—Fiction] I. Sabuda, Robert, ill.
II. Thoreau, Henry David, 1817-1862. Walden. III. Title.
PZ7.L9645Wal 1990 [E] 89-70903
ISBN 0-399-22153-0

INTRODUCTION

Henry David Thoreau was born on July 12, 1817, on his grandmother's farm outside Concord, Massachusetts. There he lived with his parents and his older sister and brother, Helen and John, until the family moved to Concord village and the children started school. Henry's father owned a pencil-making business, called The Pencil Factory, in Concord, and his mother often took boarders into the family's home to supplement their income.

Henry's mother and father enjoyed taking their children on long walks and on picnics in the nearby fields and woods. Mrs. Thoreau showed the children how to sit very still and listen to the music of the birds.

As soon as John and Helen finished school in Concord, they became teachers but Henry went on to Harvard College. Henry enjoyed school and studied French, German, Italian, and Spanish and learned to read Greek and Latin. He graduated from Harvard in 1837, just before his twentieth birthday.

After returning to Concord, Henry and his brother opened their own school, called Concord Academy. They believed that children learned better when they were enjoying what they were learning, and the school program often included walks in the fields and woods, and boating on Concord's two rivers.

In 1842 John Thoreau died suddenly, and Henry did not want to continue teaching without him. Ralph Waldo Emerson, a writer and friend, gave Thoreau some land beside Walden Pond and encouraged him to build a study in the woods and write. Thoreau built a woodshed and a one-room cabin and there he lived for "two years, two months, and two days." Inside the cabin there was a bed, a desk, a fireplace, three chairs, and a shelf for books. Thoreau wrote first a book called *A Week on the Concord and Merrimack Rivers*, about a boat trip that he and John had taken. He dedicated the book to John.

After about two years, Thoreau gave his cabin to Mr. Emerson and returned to Concord where he wrote his most famous book, *Walden*. Part of this book he first wrote in a journal that he had kept while he was living on the pond. *Walden* tells about the walks that Thoreau took in all kinds of weather, the visitors he had, and the flowers and trees and birds that he lived with. This picture-book *Walden* describes some of Thoreau's life there, but after meeting Thoreau in these pages the best place to discover more about him is in his own complete *Walden*.

Anne McGrath, The Thoreau Lyceum
Concord, Massachusetts

Near the end of March, 1845, I borrowed an axe and went down to the woods by Walden Pond, nearest to where I intended to build my house, and began to cut down some tall, arrowy white pines, still in their youth, for timber.

My purpose in going to Walden Pond was not to live cheaply nor to live dearly there, but to transact some private business with the fewest obstacles.

At length, in the beginning of May...
I set up the frame of my house.
...I laid the foundation of a chimney
at one end, bringing two cartloads
of stones up the hill from the pond
in my arms.
I began to occupy my house on
the 4th of July, as soon as it was
boarded and roofed....
Well, there I might live, I said;
and there I did live, for an hour,
a summer and a winter life.

Morning is when I am awake and there is a dawn in me.
I got up early and bathed in the pond.

Early in the morning I worked
barefooted....
Removing the weeds, putting fresh
soil about the bean stems...making
the earth say beans instead of
grass,—this was my daily work.

Sometimes, in a summer morning, having taken my accustomed bath, I sat in my sunny doorway from sunrise till noon, rapt in a revery, amidst the pines and hickories and sumachs, in undisturbed solitude and stillness, while the birds sang around or flitted noiseless through the house, until by the sun falling in at my west window, or the noise of some travellers' wagon on the distant highway, I was reminded of the lapse of time.

Regularly at half-past seven, in
one part of the summer, after the
evening train had gone by, the
whip-poor-wills chanted their
vespers for half an hour....
Sometimes I heard four or five at
once in different parts of the wood....
They would begin to sing almost
with as much precision as a clock,
within five minutes of a particular
time, referred to the setting of the
sun, every evening.

In warm evenings I frequently sat in the boat playing the flute, and saw the perch, which I seem to have charmed, hovering around me, and the moon travelling over the ribbed bottom, which was strewed with the wrecks of the forest.
I have my horizon bounded by woods all to myself.

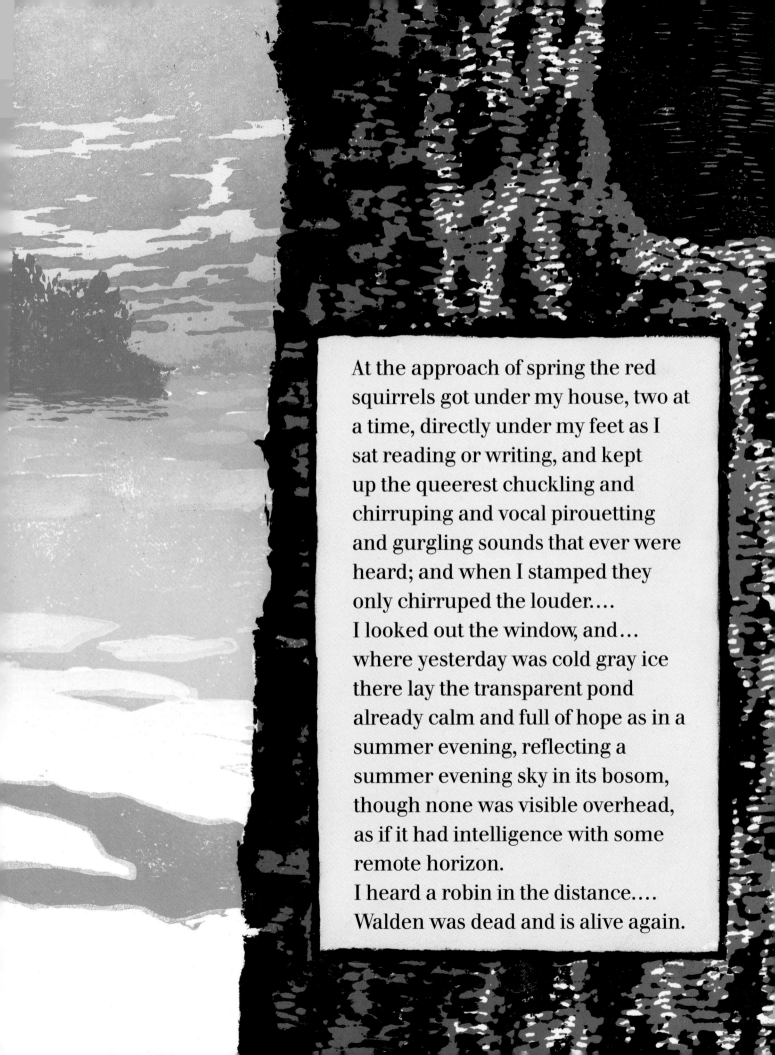

At the approach of spring the red squirrels got under my house, two at a time, directly under my feet as I sat reading or writing, and kept up the queerest chuckling and chirruping and vocal pirouetting and gurgling sounds that ever were heard; and when I stamped they only chirruped the louder....

I looked out the window, and... where yesterday was cold gray ice there lay the transparent pond already calm and full of hope as in a summer evening, reflecting a summer evening sky in its bosom, though none was visible overhead, as if it had intelligence with some remote horizon.

I heard a robin in the distance.... Walden was dead and is alive again.

Thus was my first year's life in the woods completed; and the second year was similar to it. I finally left Walden September 6th, 1847.
I left the woods for as good a reason as I went there. Perhaps it seemed to me that I had several more lives to live, and could not spare any more time for that one.

I learned this, at least, by my experiment…
Only that day dawns to which we are awake.
The sun is but a morning star.